FROM WAX
To Crayon

A Photo Essay
by Michael H. Forman

Ⅎ
Children's Press

A Division of Grolier Publishing
New York London Hong Kong Sydney
Danbury, Connecticut

Created and Developed by The Learning Source

Designed by Josh Simons

Acknowledgments: We would like to thank Binney & Smith, the producers of Crayola crayons, the Children's Aid Society, and the other organizations who provided technical assistance with this project. Their help is greatly appreciated.

Illustrations: Aliza Simons: cover, 5 (right); Casey Simons: 5 (botttom left), 30 (right); Dyani Holiday: 31 (right); Emily Egan: 1; Gabriel Barth-Maron: 30 (left); Noah Forman: 5 (top); Rachel & Ariel Ball: 31 (left); Tammy Christian: 30 (center).

Photo Credits: Binney & Smith: 2-3, 8, 10-11, 13 (right), 14-27, back cover; Ken Karp: 8 (inset), 28-29: Robert Egan: 4-7; Sun Chemical Corporation: 13 (left).

Note: The actual crayon-making process often varies from manufacturer to manufacturer. The facts and details included in this book are representative of one of the most common ways of producing crayons today.

Library of Congress Cataloging-in-Publication Data
Forman, Michael H.
        From wax to crayon / by Michael H. Forman.
                p.   cm. — (Changes)
Summary: Describes how crayons are made, inspected, wrapped, sorted, and packed for use in drawing and coloring just about anything on earth.
ISBN 0-516-20708-3 (lib. bdg.)   ISBN 0-516-20360-6 (pbk.)
        1. Crayons — Juvenile literature. [1. Crayons.] I. Title. II.
Series: Changes (New York, N.Y.)
        TS1268.F67 1997
        741.2'3—dc21
                                96-51022 CIP
                                AC
Printed in the United States of America
1 2 3 4 5 6 7 8 9 10 R 06 05 04 03 02 01 00 99 98 97

Where will your crayons take you?
Will they lead you to tall, crowded cities
or into thick, dark forests
or for visits beneath the sea?

With crayons you can travel anywhere. Just bring along your imagination and lots of different colors.

But where do crayons come from?

Crayons begin with wax. So, outside the crayon factory, tanks of clear, gooey wax stand, waiting for color.

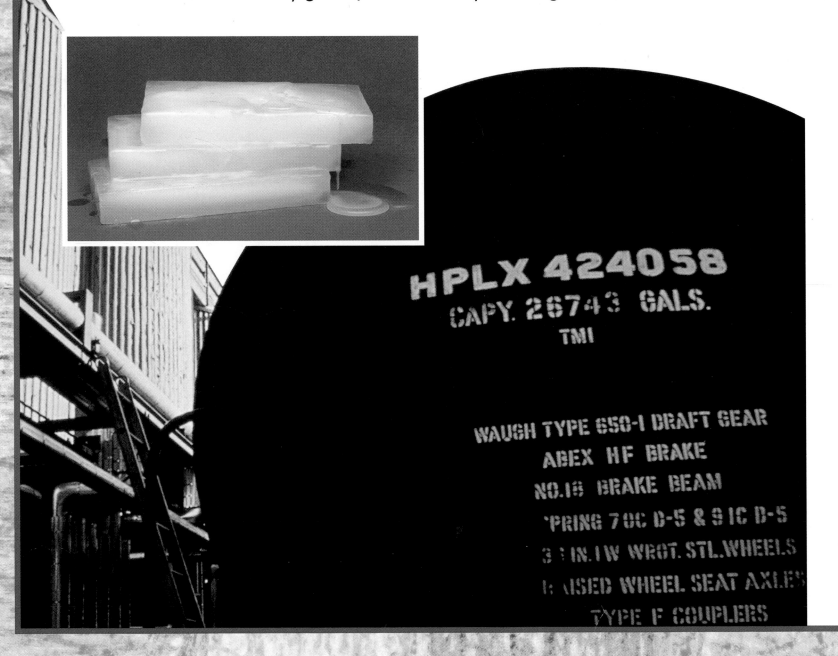

Meanwhile, at the color mill, the primary colors—
red, blue, and yellow—are made from chemicals.

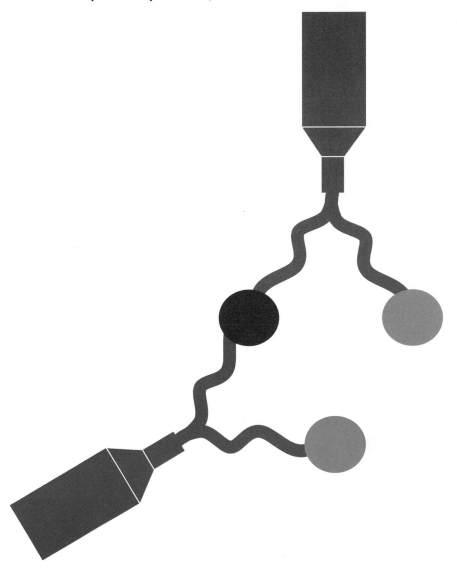

The primary colors are then mixed together in
different ways to create many other colors.

Once a color looks right, its mixture is baked in a special oven, called a kiln.

Hours later, hard color cakes are removed from the kiln . . .

. . . and ground into fine powder by a pulverizing machine.

The colored powder, called pigment, is packed into bags and sent off to the crayon factory.

There, in big vats, the pigments are mixed with very
hot, liquid wax.

Each mixture of wax and pigment must be blended over and over. Otherwise, one end of a crayon could come out a different color than the other end.

15

The newly colored wax is poured over molds and stirred to keep air bubbles from forming. A bubble inside a crayon might cause it to break later on.

Soon the wax hardens into these familiar shapes.

The crayons must cool for a while. Then they are removed from the molds . . .

. . . and checked for chips and dents. After all, no one wants new crayons that are already broken.

A machine wraps and labels each crayon . . .

. . . and boxes it with others that are exactly the same.
But hundreds of crayons of the same color aren't much fun.

So the sorter combines them into sets . . .

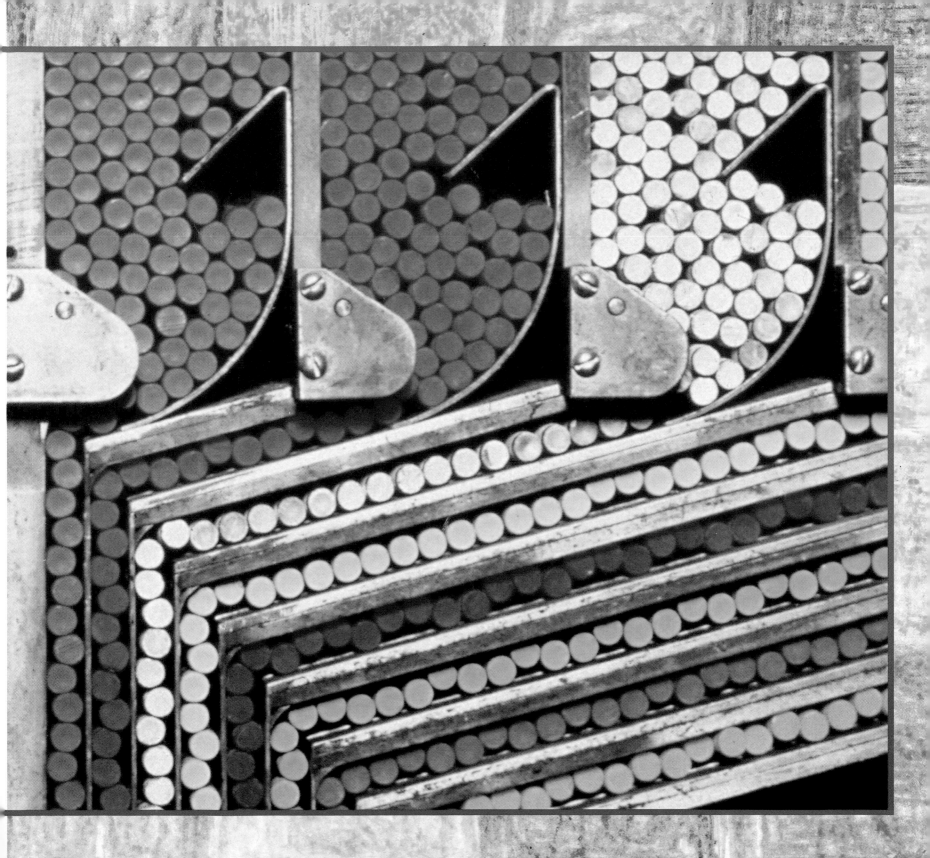

. . . with all the colors that people like to use.

At last, the crayons reach the packing machine. Here, they go into open-ended packages called sleeves . . .

. . . and then into boxes, ready for you.

29

. . . even the best-looking person you know.
And who could that be?

Here are some unusual crayon names.
Can you think of any others?

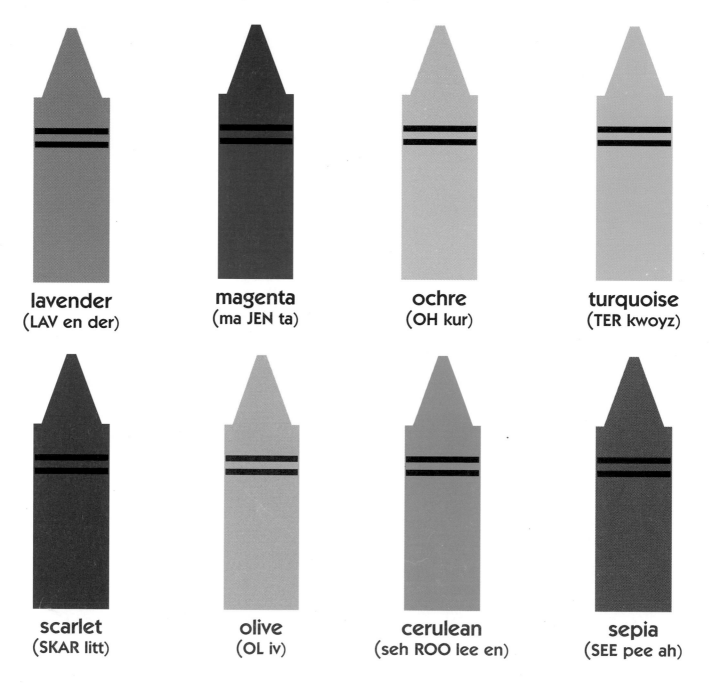

lavender
(LAV en der)

magenta
(ma JEN ta)

ochre
(OH kur)

turquoise
(TER kwoyz)

scarlet
(SKAR litt)

olive
(OL iv)

cerulean
(seh ROO lee en)

sepia
(SEE pee ah)